HAÑA ZÜKI

Book *of* Treasures

THE OFFICIAL GUIDE

by Brandon T. Snider

Abrams Books For Y
• New Yo

Cataloging-in-Publication Data has been applied for and may
be obtained from the Library of Congress.

ISBN 978-1-4197-2933-1

Book design by Laura Crescenti and Pamela Notarantonio

Printed and bound in U.S.A.
10 9 8 7 6 5 4 3 2 1

Abrams Books for Young Readers are available at special
discounts when purchased in quantity for premiums and promotions
as well as fundraising or educational use. Special editions can
also be created to specification. For details, contact
specialsales@abramsbooks.com or the address below.

ABRAMS The Art of Books
195 Broadway, New York, NY 10007
abramsbooks.com

Out there, deep in space
Grows a new Moonflower
That blooms in every way
When she treasures her moods
She finds her power
To discover a new day
HANAZUKI
Moods flowing
HANAZUKI
Her colors are showing
HANAZUKI
Powers her world

When she listens within
She can light up the sky
With pure emotion
Sharing all her magic Treasures
Moods changing by the hour
With her friends
She's a true Moonflower

Saving the day
With no time to waste
HANAZUKI
Moods flowing
HANAZUKI
Her colors are showing
HANAZUKI
Powers her world

HANAZUKI
Moods flowing
HANAZUKI
Her colors are showing
HANAZUKI
Powers her world

This is going to be SO MUCH FUN!

The Legend of the
MOONFLOWER

IN a distant galaxy, super-duper crazy far away from *everything*, sits a cluster of colorful moons unlike anything anyone has ever seen before! These aren't boring moons covered in dusty old craters. These moons are kaleidoscopes of color, full of all kinds of bright, shiny life. And they're in great danger. A dark force is sweeping through the cosmos, sucking all the color from every moon it encounters. The worst part is that no one knows what this force wants other than to destroy stuff. They call it the **BIG BAD**.

Each moon has a Moonflower who protects it from the Big Bad. Like Me!

Protecting a moon is a big job, but Moonflowers don't work alone. Every day, Little Dreamer, this sweet snoozy guy from who knows where, brings each Moonflower a Treasure— sometimes two! When a Moonflower faces a challenge that triggers a true emotion, she glows with the color of that mood, and if she's holding a Treasure, it glows, too!

The glowing Treasure tunnels into the ground and grows into a Treasure Tree filled with brand-new Treasures! The more trees the better. They combine their energy to create a protective force field that protects the moon from the Big Bad! But Treasure Trees can only grow if Moonflowers let themselves feel their feelings. Their moods are their power!

Wacky

Scared

Neutral

Mellow

Courageous

Whew! That was an emotional roller coaster!

I'm still kinda new to this Moonflower gig, so I have a few things to figure out. But if there's one thing I *do* know, it's all about ME . . . and my moods! Take a look . . .

Happy

ME AND MY MOON

First, how about a name?
Mine's Hanazuki! At least that's
what that pyramid with a face told me,
and that guy seems like someone
I can trust! It's a pleasure to
meet you. *Officially.*

I'll be guiding you on an exciting journey across a vast celestial wonderland. You'll see my home, meet my friends, and there might even be a surprise or two if you play your cards right. You feelin' lucky? **WINK!**

We're going to have so much fun that I might explode! But not in a gross way. At least, I don't think so. The truth is, I'm learning just about anything can happen here on my moon, sweet moon. Speaking of which, this is my moon. Whaddaya think? Isn't it beauuuuutiful?

Not too long ago, when I first burst from that rainbow and became a full-fledged Moonflower, everything was so overwhelming! All the sweet smells, the glowing rivers of color, and the sweet squishies—and not-so-sweet squishies! **I. LOVED. EVERYTHING!** Even though I had **NO** idea what was going on.

Now that I've been around a little while, I've discovered that some days are better than others. That's just the plain ol' truth. Some days are full of good times and unicorns. Well, every day's full of at least *one* unicorn . . . Other days are just hard. Even though I've got pals, it can be lonely out here in the middle of the galaxy. But then I look around at this beautiful moon and all there is to see and do, and I know it's going to be OK. I'll figure it out one unicorn day at a time!

Speaking of my pals, I don't want to get too far along without introducing you to my friends!

That's my cuuuuuuuuue! Here I am, your bestie best and personal hero—

Well, I wouldn't go quite THAT far—

Dazzlessence Jones!

Isn't he a gem?

Q: *What's your greatest fear?*

A: *My friends having an amazing time
without me.*

Q: *What's your favorite color?*

A: *All of them!*

Q: *What do you do when you're not busy?*

A: *Tend to my mood garden.*

Q: *If you could live anywhere in the galaxy,
where would it be?*

A: *Right here, on this moon, surrounded
by my friends.*

Q: *What's your favorite mood?*

A: *All of them!*

FIND YOUR MOOD POWER,
Moonflower!

YOU BET I WILL!
Now let's meet everyone else.

LITTLE DREAMER!!! Or, as I like to call him, Li'l Snoozy Guy (that's our private joke). When we first met, I didn't know his name and, since he was such a floaty sleepyhead, I called him Li'l Snoozy Guy. Ahhhhh, memories!

Little Dreamer's the cute little buddy who brings me Treasures each day. He's not much of a talker, but that's OK, because I am! Still, I do wonder where he comes from, and where he goes when he zips off into space. He's pretty much a mystery, cuddling an enigma, wrapped in a toasty conundrum!

Sounds delicioussssss!

But he always shows up just when I need him most. And he always shows up in the most **AMAZING** clothes! Like this:

Badgers . . . mmmmurmmm murmmm . . . frosting . . .

I've got lots of questions for you, Snoozy.

GROW.

HOLD UP!!!! Did he just say *grow*? What does that *mean*?

Hanazuki, sometimes things are better left unknown. And sometimes it's better to discover things for yourself.

LITTLE DREAMER'S LOOKS

Shark

Clouds

Tiger

Bubbles

Aviator

Bull

Hearts

LITTLE DREAMER'S LOOKS, PART 2

Love

Stars

Dessert

Rainbow

Bee

Li'l Devil

Strawberry

THE HEMKA

AHHHH! My cushy, squeezy, irresistible little yum buckets! What would I do without these kissable softies? I'd wilt! And cry! Then I'd sulk around all day and night, missing them *so much*. Thinking about them makes my heart flutter.

Breathe, Hanazuki. In and out.

On the day I was born, the Hemka were just about the first things I saw. We loved each other immediately, and I just can't imagine life without them! See their colors? They match their moods, just like mine! Each Hemka can feel *all* the feels, but they have one *true* emotion that outshines all the rest.

The Hemka can be hard to communicate with sometimes. And yes, they're pretty much *always* getting into trouble.

Draaaammmaaaaaa!

But I just adore these little squishies. They're totally too cute for words! Wanna meet them?

Say no.

PINK HEMKA

Pink is caring, friendly, devoted, kind, and overflowing with sweetness. He's kind of like a long-eared cupcake. Pink gives the tightest hugs I've ever had! I haven't been around that long, but still, I know my way around a tight hug.

BLUE HEMKA

Little Blue is a sensitive soul. He just cares so much! When Blue is down in the dumps, he doesn't hide it, he lets it flow. And that's when I know to give him a little TLC.

RED HEMKA

Red's feisty passion is good for the soul, but when he flies off the handle, he can lose sight of what's important. We're both learning to channel our fiery energy for good!

YELLOW HEMKA

You know how, when you wake up to the sound of pyramids singing and the happy babbling of rainbow streams, you just know it's going to be a great day? That's Yellow! Full of joy and light, Yellow is just bursting with good feeling. But Yellow can be a little oblivious sometimes. Sometimes he doesn't see the Chicken Plant for the trees.

PURPLE HEMKA

Stand tall, be brave, take no prisoners! Purple is an adventurous soul who charges into things without a second thought. Or a third. Or fourth. First one to help, last one to leave, you definitely want Purple on your team. You just might want to put someone else in charge.

LIME GREEN HEMKA

Lime Green is always on edge, but that's just because he's so worried about his friends! There's a lot to be afraid of out there, and LG is afraid of it all. But when there's a challenge to be faced, you can count on Lime Green to find the safest solution.

21

ORANGE HEMKA

Orange is totally OUT THERE! Just look at those eyes! Orange does his own thing, his own way, and he doesn't care what anyone thinks! It's what I love most about him. Orange's worst fear is getting eaten by a giant space whale—totally weird because giant space whales only eat Lime Green Hemka!

GREEN HEMKA

Hey. 'Sup. How's it goin'? Cool. Cool. Me? I'm totally chiiiiiiiilllll.

That was my impression of Green Hemka. Pretty good, right? (Thanks for saying so.) Green's so laid back, sometimes it seems like he doesn't care about anything at all. (But I know he actually cares a lot.)

LAVENDER HEMKA

That Lavender Hemka—what an inspiration! He's full of good ideas, but sometimes he's a little too shy to share them.

TEAL HEMKA

Well, well, well. If it isn't the most charismatic Hemka this side of the moon! Teal's confidence is pretty great, but sometimes he likes himself a little too much. On the other hand, he is a very likable guy.

RAINBOW HEMKA

Oh, Rainbow. He's the most emotional guy of all. He feels everything—all at once, all the time! Not only does he feel his own feelings, but he can feel yours, too! So much power! That's why you rarely see him. It's all a little too much.

So, that's everyone! At least, that's all the Hemka I've met so far. My MOST favorite thing about them? They are who they are. They're cute and (mostly) cuddly, and strong in their own ways. Kinda like me! Sometimes our powerful moods get us into trouble, but we wouldn't be us without them.

27

SLEEPY UNICORN

Secret's out! Sleepy Unicorn's the one who makes my unicorn days! He's the most-sleepiest unicorn of all time! I'll never forget the day we met. I was so stressed since I'd just **SAT ON LITTLE BLUE!** Sleepy helped me out with a little bit of his magic, even though he doesn't like using it much.

Sleepy Unicorn's horn projects his dreams, which are just about the only clues we've got to his seeecret paaaaast. Lean in.

Sleepy was once a sweet little unicorn Alterling (like a Hemka, but from a different moon), until he figured out how to use his magic to power up and become a full-sized talker named **NOBLE UNICORN.** His brother evolved into a bad guy named **TWISTED UNICORN** and led the other unicorns in a revolt against their Moonflower. Noble tried to protect his Moonflower and their moon, but Twisted's dark magic was just too strong. He took over the moon, and their Moonflower retreated to a creepy grove of dark trees, allowing the Big Bad to take over. Noble Unicorn fled to my moon for safekeeping, and *that's* when he became Sleepy.

He doesn't like talking about his past much. I don't blame him. It's scary, and a little sad! That's why I make sure to tell Sleepy Unicorn how much we all love him.

SLEEPY WORDS OF WISDOM:
"Magic should only
be used by the pure
of heart."

zzzZZZZZZ

DAZZLESSENCE JONES

And now it's time for . . .

HOLD UP, HANAZUKI! I can handle my own business. Diiig?

Um, OK! It's your time to shine, Dazzlessence!

I'm DAZZLESSENCE JONES, MOON PROTECTOR AND GUARDIAN OF THE SAFETY CAVE. I'm here to keep the peace by enforcing the rules. Rules are NOT for fools. I repeat: Rules are NOT for fools. **Rules are NOOOOOOT for FOOOOOOOOOOOOOLS! (They keep us safe!)**

The guy knows what he's talking about.

Not only am I trained in slow sand rescue—it's an abstract concept—I'm also funky tough. That means I can break it down while laying out truth bombs. I'm also a singer and a dancer who's working to become A TRIPLE THREAT. Don't cross me on the dance floor. Here's why: DANCE BREAK.

Jiggle that jelly! FOR JUSTICE!

Hey, Dazzy J, who's Dazzlessence Jackson?

WHAT?! STOP THE MUSIC.
Where did you hear that name?!

Oh. Um. He appeared to us when we were in the Volcano of Fears!

NO QUESTIONS! Right now, it's official moon business ONLY. Here's what you need to know: BE CAREFUL WHEN YOU'RE ON THE DARK SIDE OF THE MOON. It's not always safe over there.

BE CAREFUL OF 213s (that's code for meteor showers). They can happen at any time. See a shower, shout about 'er! Then I'll call in a 412 (that's code for a Hemka formation) to execute a 218 (that's code for clearing meteors from an area) and we'll get the situation handled ASAP.

Isn't he just the best diamond ever? Dazzlessence is a shimmering beacon of hope to everyone around him. The galaxy could use as much of that as possible.

CHICKEN PLANT

Chicken Plant is not your friend.

Sure she is! Sort of . . .

GRUMPY WORDS OF WISDOM:

"Nothing on this planet
agrees with my stomach!"

CHICKEN PLANT is exactly what you think! (That is to say she's a chicken who is also a plant.) She can be gruff, grumpy, and mean-spirited, but be nice to her. She's been through a lot! A little affection might just give her the push she needs to change her . . . challenging ways. Or not. Who can tell? She's exhausting.

Want to hear how I met Chicken Plant? Gather round, because this is a good one. **PICTURE IT:** I was strolling along peacefully (as one does) after tending to a sick Treasure Tree. All of a sudden, Little Dreamer popped up out of nowhere. Classic Little Dreamer! He dropped a Treasure in front of me and floated away. Then, when I was distracted thinking about where Little Dreamer goes when he's not dropping Treasures in front of me, I was startled by a talking animal plant thingie! It was Chicken Plant!

Once we got to gabbing, it was like we were old friends. Kind of. Maybe. OK, I'll admit, we got off to a rocky start when Chicken Plant started eating Hemka. But we worked it all out! Even though she's cranky, rude, and eats Hemka, I still love Chicken Plant!

Chicken Plant lays a lot of weird eggs. One hatched into a Baby Chicken Plant that kept running around like a Chicken Plant with its head cut off (but its head was fine, stop worrying!). Another time, Chicken Plant hatched a buggy little baby that we called **JUNIOR**. He had the cutest little crab arms and horrifying spider face! Then he kept gobbling up Treasure Trees, changing colors every time he ate one! His body kept growing, but his brain stayed baby-sized. Eventually, he floated away and it made Chicken Plant so sad. She expressed her sadness by being mean, but I knew how she felt. I let her know it was OK to feel her true feelings. We've been better friends ever since.

She used to call me Zookahoney. Ahhhhh, memories!

DOUGHY BUNINGTON

DOUGHY BUNINGTON! What a delightful bunch of pudge.
LOOK AT THAT FACE. I want to lather it up in a sweet sauce and
EAT IT. I won't, though. He's a softy who just wants to be loved.
DON'T WE ALL? He's also a bit of a crier, which is OK! A good
cry is good for you, and since Doughy cries once a day at least,
he must be the healthiest hot-dog-in-a-bun creature to ever
live on the Dark Side of the Moon.

Doughy's hobbies include tasting things, eating snacks, and
finding the right flavor combinations. He can also speak to and
understand Treasure Trees, which has been a **BIG** help. You have
no idea. I'm grateful to have a guy like Doughy on Team Hanazuki.

Now, I've never told anyone this, so I hope you can keep
a secret. One time, Doughy licked my arm! He thought it was
a long donut. It was one of the weirdest days of my life.

Hot tip: Do NOT bring up Chicken Plant around Doughy.
They have what we in the Moonflower business call a beef.
It means they're not exactly the best of friends. One time,
Doughy ate Chicken Plant's wings. It was an accident! I think.
That's why Doughy was exiled to the Dark Side of the Moon.
SIGH. What can I say? Stuff happens. But I won't stop trying to
get them to hug it out!

Mistaaaaaaaaake!!

Oh, and one more thing!
Doughy might just be the key
to saving the galaxy!

DOUGHY WORDS OF WISDOM:

"Oh, crackers!"

BASIL GANGLIA is my favorite amorphous brain in a cave! I met him when I traveled to the Dark Side of the Moon. He's a schemer. Surprise! I mean, he looks like a schemer, but I don't like to judge a book by its cover. And I don't like to judge a brain with eyes by how frightening it looks. It's unfair and, frankly, rude. **MY POINT IS:** Be careful around him. He might try to manipulate you into building him a spacesurfer, which he'll then use to take off to some other moon because he can't rule this one.

When I first met Basil, I was in total awe. It felt like destiny, you know? People rarely come face-to-face with a brain in a cave, so I knew I must've been crazy lucky. It turns out he was stuck there, desperately hoping to escape after a failed takeover of the moon. With no arms or legs, he relied on other folks to do everything, and they failed him. **BEEN THERE, GUY!**

Basil was once my moon's greatest mastermind, communicating with brains on other moons through something he calls the **ECNYWYWAPO** (Elite Cerebral Network You Wish You Were a Part Of). I'm not exactly sure what that is, but gosh do I wish I were a part of it.

He's a rude dude with a nasty 'tuuuuuude.

Who still deserves our love and affection because everyone is struggling with something.

BASIL WORDS OF WISDOM:

"Do not test me!
I am a legless brain!"

Scattered on the surface of my moon are so many curious things—it'll leave you asking, "Did that monolith just ask me a question?" (Spoiler alert—it did!) Let's review some of my planetoid's most marvelous spectacles.

When you talk to **MIRROR PLANT**, it repeats what you say! Easy peasy, riiight? There's a catch. Mirror Plant can sense what you really mean, even if it's not what you say. In other words, she'll say your truest thoughts out loud. Not the best plant to have around when you're trying to keep a secret. That's why I love her.

MIRROR PLANT

TALKING MOUNTAIN

This is a TALKING MOUNTAIN.
It's . . . a mountain that talks.

Better than a Chicken Plant,
that's for sure.

SLOW SAND

Here's some slow sand. It's everywhere!

You step in that stuff, and you're a goner. It'll take a long time to swallow you, but eventually it'll getcha!

MOUTH PORTAL

MOUTH PORTAL is an enormous—you guessed it—mouth portal. But it doesn't say much, which is very weird. I should look into the why of that. If you need a quick way to get from the Light Side of the Moon to the Dark Side, just hop on through! I think it also goes to other dimensions, too (I should put that on my list of things to confirm). Oh, and it gently blows away other moons and dangerous things that get too close. Except for the **BIG BAD**. I think. I should really do my research!

That thing is freeeeeeaky. But helpful.

THE VOLCANO OF FEARS

Poor souls who are unfortunate enough to enter **THE VOLCANO OF FEARS** are faced with their worst, most horrifying fears over and over again.

> **I DON'T WANT TO TALK ABOUT THE VOLCANO OF FEARS. It's too . . . what's the word? SCARY.**

Plus—**IT'S A VOLCANO**. Talk about a double whammy. Let's move on . . .

· TALKING PYRAMID ·

This is a **TALKING PYRAMID.**
It's . . . a pyramid that talks.

His left eye is the good one!

43

THE LIGHT AND DARK SIDES OF THE MOON

This is the Light Side of the Moon. Ahhhhhh! Some days I just run around and thank the stars I live on such a beautiful planetoid. Look at all this lusciousness. I can have fun and express my mood without fear. It's GOOD to be a Moonflower.

We are LUUUUUUCKY. On the Light Side, we do things right. I hate to burst your bubble, but it's time to peek at the Dark Side and see what's happening.

Burst away, Dazzlessence Jones.

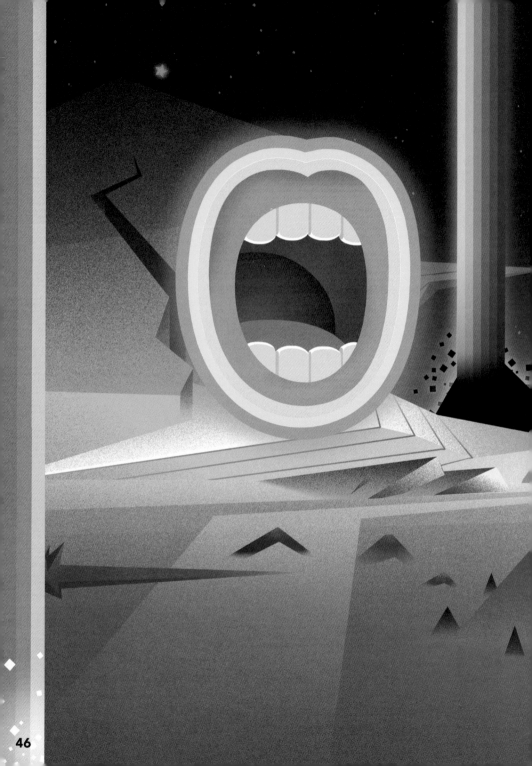

Here it is. The Dark Side of the Moon. LoOKs peaceful, doesn't it?

It looks peaceful, but it's not a place I want to live, that's for sure. It isn't exactly the scary, dangerous place that I used to think it was way back when I first got here, but it's still questionable. And without any Treasure Trees, it's definitely not where I want to be when the **BIG BAD** makes its move.

All I see are violations! That bubbling goop loOKs crime-ridden. And those cupcake and donut trees need pruning.

I'm sure Doughy Bunington will take care of those. He's a hungry boy! And a messy boy. Is he a boy? I can't tell under all that dough. Oh well. I think I'm ready to head back to the Light Side now. Home is always where I feel the safest.

You got it.

FORCES OF DARKNESS

It's time to get serious.

Out there? In the galaxy? There are some scary things lurking around. Hiding in the dark reaches of the cosmos are a TON of nutty bad guys with issues. Yeesh. I shouldn't say that! I'm sure some bad guys are very nice when you get to know them. The bottom line is that a Moonflower has to know what they're up against.

Let's meet the FORCES OF DARKNESS, shall we?

THE BIG BAD

ALL HANDS ON DECK! I REPEAT, ALL HANDS ON DECK! THE BIG BAD IS COMING AND WE'VE GOT TO BE **PREPARED!**

A wise friend once said: Breathe in, breathe ooooooouuuuuuuttttttt.

Don't worry, The BIG BAD isn't here just yet. We're safe. *For now.*

No one is sure where the **BIG BAD** came from. No one knows what it wants, either (other than to bleed moons dry of color and life and then destroy them). It's out there, slowly creeping up on unsuspecting moons.

When I first saw the **BIG BAD**, I felt a chill go up my spine. That's what happens when a slithering black sludge creature rains down from the sky and sucks the life out of the universe. Why does this thing want to destroy stuff? Who knows? Probably because someone was mean to it one time and now it wants to be mean to **EVERYTHING**. I do know one thing, we can't give up **HOPE**.

Some moons can withstand the **BIG BAD**'s attack. Their secret? **TREASURE TREES**. Fill a moon with Treasure Trees, and it won't look like one big delectable midnight snack. I've been doing my best, but it hasn't been easy.

TWISTED UNICORN

TWISTED UNICORN is a mean and powerful bully who rules his moon with an iron hoof! He's also Sleepy Unicorn's brother, remember? I feel like we've already said this guy's name more than he deserves.

Truth!

Twisted Unicorn uses **DARK MAGIC** to control his Little Unicorn minions like cute little puppets who you want to hug and snuggle and love and treasure and play with and rub your nose on and giggle with and . . .

KEEP IT TOGETHER, H!

Twisted invented a Rainbow Dome to protect his moon from the **BIG BAD**, but it's just an excuse to keep his Little Unicorns busy. That way they don't have time to realize how miserable they are. **UGH**. What a sad life.

I'll always hold out hope that one day Twisted Unicorn comes to his senses and stops being a terrifying intergalactic despot. It's my dream (one of **MANY**) that he'll show up on my moon and say, "Sorry I was such a meanie, I need love. Can a unicorn get a **HUG** up in here?" Then I'll say, "Come'ere, friend. These arms were made for hugging." Then we'll laugh and laugh and laugh.

You've got strange dreams, girl.

MAZZADRIL ATTACK! THIS IS NOT A DRILL!

The Mazzadril are scary. Like REALLY scary. After the BIG BAD wiped out Kiazuki's moon, the Mazzadril ran wild. THAT'S how scary they are. Mazzadril are monstrous creatures that cause chaos and destruction wherever they go. On my moon, they mostly live on the creepy Dark Side. Kiazuki showed me that Mazzadril can be defeated by the fruit of the black Treasure Trees.

And Chicken Plant Junior!

That's right! I miss that little guy.

MEET THE OTHER MOONFLOWERS

Turns out, I'm not the only Moonflower in the galaxy. Some of the others have been around a looooong time, and they've seen a lot of crazy stuff. We've all got lessons to share with one another. That's the only way we'll ever figure out how to defeat the BIG BAD. So get a load of this . . .

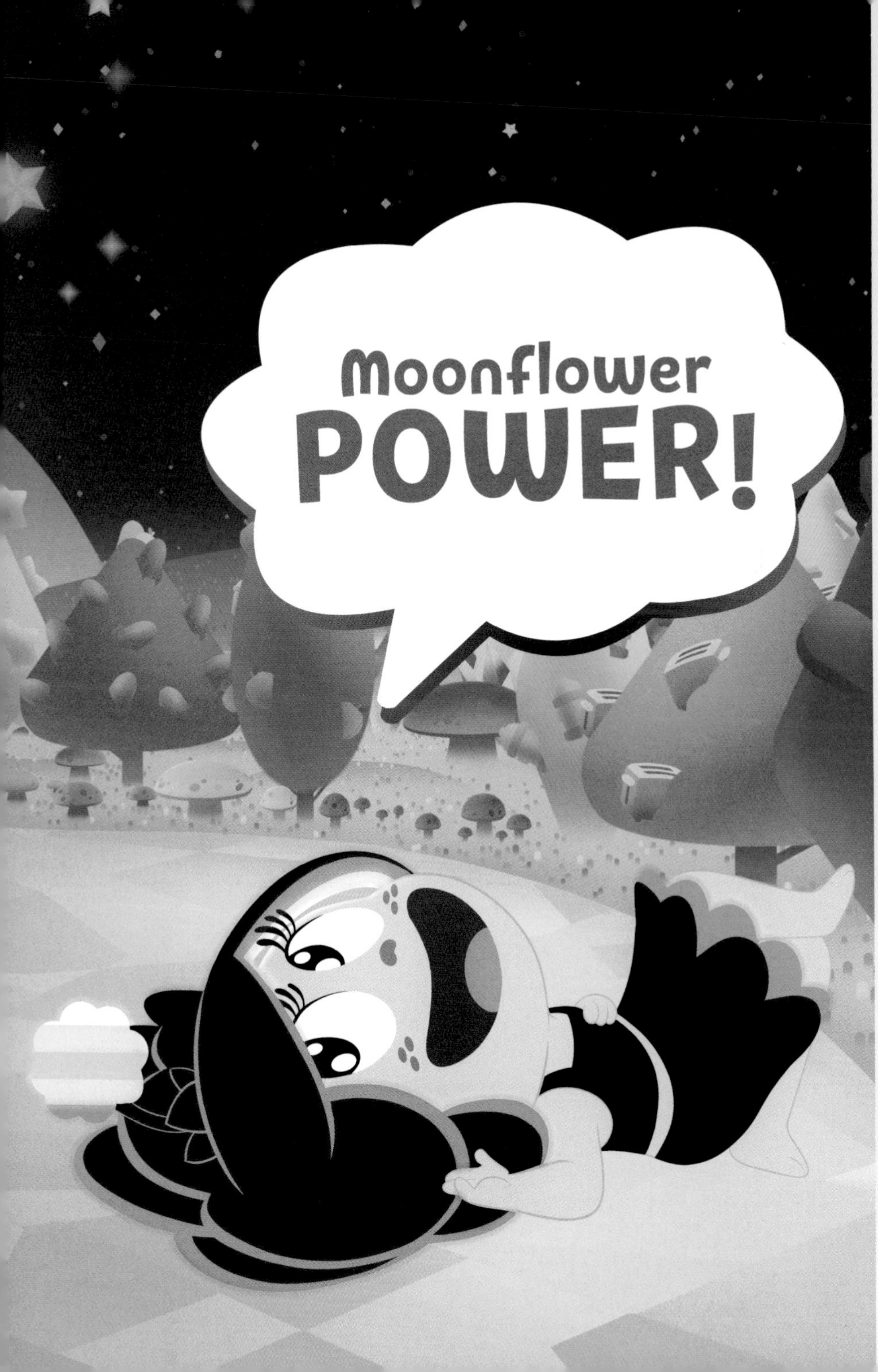
Moonflower POWER!

Well, well, well. WHAT. HAVE. WE. HERE?

JK. I'm being dramatic. I know exactly what we have here: **KIAZUKI!** She's a Moonflower, too. But we're pretty different, ol' Kiazuki and I. For one thing, she doesn't seem to like to have fun. I suppose she's got her reasons.

Kiazuki has been a Moonflower longer than I've been alive, and her moon is, to put it bluntly, a drab wasteland filled with misery, uncertainty, and a sense of impending doom. It used to be bright and colorful like mine, but the **BIG BAD** came and took all the color away. It took Kiazuki's color away too, leaving her angry and bitter. Sometimes Little Dreamer brings Treasures for Kiazuki, but she can't make them grow. This makes her feel even **WORSE!** But except for being mad all the time, Kiazuki doesn't seem to want to let her true feelings show. I'm trying to show her that being honest about her feelings is the only way to turn Treasures into Treasure Trees! Getting this through Kiazuki's head has been an uphill battle, *and I'm not wearing hiking boots.*

> That was a good jooooooooooooOKAHHHHHH!

I absolutely, 100 percent, no doubt whatsoever, consider Kiazuki a sister and a friend, buuuuuut I learned the hard way **NOT** to try giving her a high five. She hates 'em. You'll just end up with your hand in the air for hours, waiting for that sweet, sweet slap. **SIGH.**

AND ANOTHER THING I SHOULD MENTION. Kiazuki used to ride the cosmic winds on her spacesurfer, traveling to other moons to organize Moonflowers across the galaxy. They became friends and supported one another. She called them **THE GARLANDIANS**. Doesn't that sound majestic and important? Oh, and when her moon was attacked, no one came to help Kiazuki. That hurt my heart. She wouldn't tell me why, but I suspect that's just another reason she's down all the time.

This is Kiazuki's pet, **ZIKORO**. More on him later.

This is Kiazuki's **SPACESURFER**. Isn't it sleek? She's good at cobbling stuff together since she's had to scrape and scratch just to survive.

KIYOSHI has been there, done that, gone into hiding, come back out, and now he's ready to tackle life with renewed vigor! I'd like to think I had a little part in that. He was once the Moonflower of Sleepy Unicorn's moon.

Remember *that* drama?

They were pals like Sleepy and I are now. When Twisted Unicorn and his mischievous Little Unicorns revolted, Kiyoshi went into hiding by retreating into a **BLACK TREASURE TREE FOREST**. Here's the thing about Black Treasure Trees: They don't protect against the **BIG BAD AT ALL**. They're grown from feelings of shame and despair. Those were the only kind of Treasure Trees Kiyoshi could grow. It breaks my heart just thinking about it.

When Kiyoshi first came out of hiding, we didn't see things eye-to-eye. We still don't, if you want to know the truth (and I'm almost positive you do). It's taken him time to get back into the swing of things, but, with a little help from his old pal Sleepy Unicorn, Kiyoshi is making progress! He just needed people to believe in him. He's still anxious and moody, but, in time, he'll be an exceptional Moonflower. **I CAN FEEL IT**.

MEEEEEE TOOOOOO!

Do you ever get the feeling Kiyoshi has some extra magical something?

Definitely! I love a mystery!

Sleepy Unicorn and I were on our way back home after a trip to his moon (where we met Kiyoshi) when suddenly we were bombarded with **EXPLODING moon DEBRIS!** That's when **MAROSHI** showed up and saved us. All that debris was from **HIS moon**. Maroshi came from a water-based moon, and when the **BIG BAD** froze it completely, it caused pressure to build inside the moon's watery core, until finally . . . **BOOM!** It exploded. You can probably still find pieces of it in space. **OooOooO** space rocks! Thankfully, Maroshi got out in time.

While Sleepy and I were away, Maroshi had been hanging out on my moon, befriending my friends and basically **REPLACING ME IN THEIR LIVES**. I wasn't happy. Oh, and all that moon debris? It fell to the surface and destroyed all my Treasure Trees. I was angry at Maroshi for a while. **I'M NOT PROUD OF THAT**. But Moonflowers are family. We stick together, forgive one another, and laugh in the face of danger. **HA! HA HA! HA! HA! HA! HAHAHAHAHAHAHAHAHA!**

(I THINK HANAZUKI'S LOSING IT.)

Yeah, maybe I am.
It's been a long journey.

ALTERLINGS

It's time to meet the **ALTERLINGS**. They're the little buddies who live on all the moons and help Moonflowers grow. **GAZE UPON THESE DARLINGS**.

Oh no. Oh nonononono. My head is spinning. I think I might pass out from **CUTE OVERLOAD**. Dazzlessence Jones, do the breathing thing! **DO THE BREATHING THING!!**

LITTLE UNICORNS are delightful bundles of bliss, scampering about their world, assisting their leader and one another. Sleepy Unicorn used to be one before his **TRANSFORMATION**. Little Unicorns are peaceful creatures unless they turn naughty and become **ROGUE UNICORNS!** That's what happened when Twisted pushed his Little Unicorn army too hard. They'd been using their horns to maintain a protective dome around their moon until one day they **SNAPPED** and began fighting with one another and causing trouble for Twisted. They didn't like that he made them work their hooves to the bone, so they rebelled against him and went rogue. **YAY** for standing up for yourself! **NAY** for being trapped in a bad situation.

If the **FLOCHI** were train conductors (go with me here), that train would be called the **SNUGGLE EXPRESS**, because **LOOK AT THESE SMILEY BOYS**. Maroshi is so lucky to be surrounded by this sweetness. Flochi are excellent at following directions and working together as a group. Well, maybe not all of them. Wanderer tends to do his own thing, which, truth be told, I think is awesome. I love an independent spirit!

This is **ZIKORO**, Kiazuki's snarling little companion. He can be cute when he's not growling, slobbering, or acting like a meanie. Awwww, I think he's just shy. And angry. And hungry. And his teeth are sharp. And he howls at the moon constantly. And he's a bad influence on the Hemka. But, otherwise, he's a peach! Since the Big Bad decimated Kiazuki's world, Zikoro is probably the last of his kind.

Or maybe not . . .

Kiazuki has a bad habit of taking her frustration out on Zikoro, which is not nice by any means, especially since he'd do anything for her. GIVE AN ANGRY PUP A BREAK ALREADY.

Always make sure your Alterlings are registered with your Moon's Bureau of Alterling Development and Safety. It's the riiiiiight thiiiiiing to dooooooooooo!

Well, now that you know everything there is to know—
YOU don't even know everything there is to know!
How would you like to learn how to be a Moonflower?
This ought to be good . . .

MOOD BOARD!
.... LAVENDER ....

*So! The best way to be a Moonflower is to learn how to tap into all your most emotional emotions. Let's start with **INSPIRED**.*

Use the space below to explore some big ideas—don't be shy!

Let's get started!
What's something that inspires you?

_____

_____

_____

_____

Remember the last great idea you had?
What was it?

_____

_____

_____

_____

If you could invent any plant at all—anything you can imagine! —to grow on your moon, what would it look like?

Draw me a picture!

HOW TO GROW A TREASURE TREE

STEP 1
Be a Moonflower.
(I believe in you!)

STEP 2
Accept a small
Treasure from
Little Dreamer.

STEP 3
Express an
authentic mood.
That mood will
give you power.

STEP 4

Note the moment when your small Treasure begins to glow.

STEP 5

Toss the small Treasure on the ground where there's room for a Tree to grow.

STEP 6

MAKE ROOM.

STEP 7

And finally . . .

CARING FOR YOUR NEW TREASURE TREE

You did it! You grew a Treasure Tree! You're *so together*!

But, um, how exactly did . . . you . . . do . . . that? Are you already a Moonflower? Or maybe you're just an amazing person who can do anything they put their mind to. No big deal.

Here are some things to keep in mind as you cherish your Treasure Tree for centuries to come! (Provided the **BIG BAD** doesn't destroy the galaxy first, which it won't! **DUH!**)

- Sweet talk! Trees love to be told how scrumptious they look.

- Pretend it's the only tree in the galaxy. That way it'll feel super-special.

- Give it LOVE. *That's how things grow, silly.*

- Don't you overpick it, or you'll put your entire moon in danger!

- Remind the Hemka not to overpick it either. *They'll put your entire moon in danger!*

- If your tree looks a little wilted, give it some food to make it strong. Icky sticky goop works nicely.

- Celebrate its beautiful life every single day!

... watch your Treasure Tree grow big and strong!

MOOD BOARD!
·········· LIME GREEN ··········

You know, I'm having a blast with you,
but I can't help thinking about the **BIG BAD**.
It's always in the back of my mind.

WHA—DID YOU HEAR THAT?
I sure am on edge today, fully
feeling my **FEAR**.

Can you think of times when it's
fun to be afraid? Because I sure
could use a little fun right about now . . .

_____

_____

_____

Hey, that worked!
Let's keep going . . .

What makes you feel safe?
Draw a picture of something that
makes you feel protected and strong.

HOW TO KEEP YOUR HEMKA HAPPY

Hemka can be very difficult to manage. They do what they want most of the time, even when you ask them VERY NICELY. Keeping them out of trouble is the key to being happy!
I mean, um, it's the key to keeping the Hemka happy. Heheheh.

Play games such as Stop Eating Icky Sticky Goop or If You Keep Hiding Treasures, We Won't Be Able to Grow Treasure Trees.

- Distract them with shiny objects.

- DO NOT INVITE ZIKORO OVER BECAUSE HE WILL MAKE THE HEMKA DO BAD THINGS.

- Twirl them in circles until they're dizzy and pass out.

- Challenge them to take naps. Whoever is asleep the longest wins! And the winner's prize is an even longer nap!

- Hire Dazzlessence Jones to Hemka-sit.

Nooooooo. Noooooo way!

- Have the Hemka relax in a warm tub of hot, icky, sticky goop.

- Tell them the Big Bad is nearby and see if they freak out.

- KEEP THEM AWAY FROM THE VOLCANO OF FEARS.

- Cuddle them, hug them, and tell them how much they mean to you.

MOOD BOARD!
YELLOW

Have I mentioned that taking care of a moon is a lot of work? Once I had to rescue Yellow Hemka from inside Chicken Plant's stomach! It was gross. But I was so overjoyed that Yellow was safe; it opened a brand-new part of my heart. Awwww. I feel good just thinking about it!

What makes you happy?

I've got the best idea. I'm going to take the day off! It'll be so fun! I'm in charge. Hmmm. I sure do like the sound of that. How about you?
If you could do anything you want for one whole day, what would you do?

_____

_____

_____

_____

_____

_____

_____

_____

And now for the best part! Draw the happiest thing you can think of!

HOW TO MAKE NEW FRIENDS

When I burst out of that rainbow and became a Moonflower, all I wanted were friends to keep me company and teach me about the galaxy and how to embrace my mood power. **AND KEEP 'EM COMING!** My little body was filled with so much love and energy that it put some people off. You can't just run up, squeeze a stranger, and expect them to become your best friend right away. Connecting to new people in new places can be difficult, but it's **NOT IMPOSSIBLE.** Here are some **DOs and DON'Ts** I learned along the way.

DO: Strike up a conversation about something you think you might have in common with your new friend.

DON'T: Talk their ear off about the nagging fear that your moon is about to be consumed by a cosmic entity that defies understanding.

DO: Share a personal story that's exciting and intriguing!

DON'T: Tell them all your secrets and then walk away.

DO: Ask your new friend about their favorite things.

DON'T: Describe in detail the intricacies of Basil Ganglia's pulsing brain matter.

DO: Inquire about any mutual friends you might have.

DON'T: Ask them why Chicken Plant is so mean and rude.

DO: Explain your role as a Moonflower and how much it means to you.

DON'T: Leave them all alone on your moon while you travel to another dimension.

DO: Bring your new pal into your circle of friends.

DON'T: Leave them alone with the Hemka during feeding time.

MOOD BOARD!
BLUE

Sniffle. Sniffle. Yes, I'm crying, OK? I get emotional whenever I think of the time I accidentally sat on Blue Hemka and flattened him. **WE JUST MET!** *It was terrible! Even though everything worked out fine,* **I STILL FEEL GUILTY!**

Can you think of times when you needed
a good cry-y-y-y?

_____

_____

_____

_____

_____

_____

_____

_____

_____

SNIFF! There are lots of other ways to feel better when you're feeling down. Can you think of some?

_____

_____

_____

_____

_____

_____

_____

_____

_____

_____

93

MOONFLOWER MESSAGES

"I'm so over this."
–KIAZUKI

"I'm doing my best over here!"
–HANAZUKI

"Hugs are the gateway to friendship!"
–HANAZUKI

"Hang loose, Moonflower!
You're doing great."
– MAROSHI

"You don't have to be
afraid of everything
that's different."
– HANAZUKI

"On the other side of
darkness, there's light.
Don't forget that."
– KIYOSHI

MOOD BOARD!

·············· RED ··············

Not to dwell on the past, but I got so mad when the Hemka fought over my very first Treasure. **MY VERY FIRST ONE!** *I didn't even get a chance to figure out what it was for, and Red Hemka was running off like he owned the thing!*

On the other hand, my anger and frustration did lead to my very first Treasure Tree, so I guess it wasn't all bad. Can you think of a time when getting angry or upset helped you achieve something?

_____

_____

_____

_____

How do you calm down when you're angry?

_____

_____

_____

Draw your angriest face!

Dance Party?

Oh, Dazzle J, is that your answer for everything?

Pretty much!

Woooooow. TREASURES.

> **You said it, H.**

These are all the Treasures that Little Dreamer gave me before they changed color and grew into Treasure Trees.

Popsicle! That was my first Treasure ever. Awww, it makes me think of Red Hemka and how angry I was that day.

Diamond! That's from when I met Chicken Plant for the first time.

Fire Hydrant! From when I sat on Little Blue! Why do I keep reliving that moment in my head???

> **Let it go, Hanazuki. You can't change the past.**

So many beautiful Treasures. So many beautiful memories! Cloud! Remember that whole thing with Chicken Plant Junior, Dazzlessence Jones? What a day.

It's an experience that's been buuuuuurned into my memoryyy!

CUPCAKE!

That one looks strangely familiar.

Of course it does. That was from the time you got bonked on the head and thought a bunch of meteors were your family. Then, you got trapped in a meteor landslide and I was so scared. I almost lost you! But I didn't.

Oh yeah! I remember now. That's when Billy, Devin, and Aunt Rita came to visit. Gooooooooood times!

Heh heh. Yeah. Um, sure. We sure have been through a lot together, Dazzy J. Thanks for all the friendship and stuff.

Anytime, H.

MOOD BOARD!

···· TEAL ····

Look at me! I bet you're wondering how I got all this swagger. Maybe I was born with it? Maybe it's Moonflower.

What makes you feel confident?
Tell me all about it!

_____

_____

_____

_____

_____

_____

_____

_____

_____

_____

_____

When I first met Kiyoshi, he wasn't very confident. So much bad stuff had happened that ol' Glass Half Empty just didn't believe he could turn things around. But I believed in him so hard that he started to believe in himself.

How has a friend turned your frown around?

_____

_____

_____

_____

_____

_____

_____

Don't tell her this, but you know Kiazuki's cute little foot things? (I don't even know what they're called!) Sometimes I want to wear them **SO BAD!** *They're super-cool!*

Design something to wear that would make you feel awesome!

MOOD BOARD!
·········· PURPLE ··········

Without Purple's help, I never would have been able to cross onto the Dark Side of the Moon or survive the Volcano of Fears! He reminded me (in his own special way) that I have to be brave, even when I might be a teensy bit scared.

What does it mean to be brave?

_____

_____

_____

_____

_____

Who is the bravest person you know?
What makes them brave?

_____

_____

_____

_____

_____

Feeling fearless! I'm going to venture to the Dark Side of the Moon to battle a Mazzadril. Don't try and stop me! I'm on a roll.

What's a fear that you've learned to overcome? How did you do it?

_____

_____

_____

_____

_____

_____

_____

Being brave is more than just standing up for what's right. It's about making good decisions. That requires thoughtfulness. Be brave! And thoughtful. Trust me on this one.

Draw yourself as a superhero!

PATIENCE, PLEASE

Everyone has problems, even though *some* people like to pretend they don't. **I'M NOT TALKING ABOUT ANYONE IN PARTICULAR**. That's how rumors start. No one is perfect. Everyone has moods, and sometimes those moods conflict with one another. So, what do you do when that happens? I'm glad you asked! Instead of acting impulsively, **HAVE PATIENCE**. I've heard it's a virtue. Take a moment to clear your head and approach things calmly and rationally. It'll help! **TRUST ME**.

How about a role-playing exercise to make things clearer?

I've got you covered!

SITUATION: Let's say a Moonflower arrives on your moon and she's got a bad attitude. You might even suspect she's working against you! What do you do?

SOLUTION: Become her friend! Sounds like she could use one. Take the time to hear what she's got to say. You might need her help one day soon.

SITUATION: Your friend, who sleeps a lot and is also a unicorn, refuses to talk about his past, even though you know that talking things out will help him get over it. What do you do?

SOLUTION: Give your friend, who sleeps a lot and is also unicorn, some space. Encourage him to speak about his past, explaining that it might help him heal. Know that it could take some time for him to share and be OK with it.

Shhhhhhh! I'm not perfect!

What's up? Let's say you and I go sit under a Treasure Tree and talk about the future. We'll chill out. No pressure. That's how Hanazuki rolls.

AHHHH! No, it's not! I'm trying to learn how to be cooler than cool from Green Hemka—nothing fazes that guy—but there's just so much to be excited about!

What do you do to keep your cool?

Keeping your cool is definitely important when you're trying to protect a moon. There are just so many things to keep track of! Treasure Trees, Little Dreamer, Chicken Plant's freaky eggs.

What's something you care about that other people don't understand? Tell me all about it!

Hmmmm. Yep. Caring is cool. I mean it isn't too cool, but, actually, yeah, yeah it is.

SITUATION: Doughy Bunington tells you he can hear and understand Treasure Trees, which is good news because you've got a bunch of Treasure Trees that feel like they've got something to say! But he's also cranky and distracted.

SOLUTION: Ask Doughy if he'd be willing to help, and offer him a treat if he does.

Hey, that's bribery.

BE WEIRD, BE YOU

Here's the thing: We're all weird, especially when we let our feelings fly! Set them free! Feel your moods!

Oh, yeah. Let 'em SHINE!

Let them color who you are, like me! That's how you'll figure out who you're truly meant to be.

Hey, Hanazuki, I've been meaning to ask you. Who are we talking to anyway?

THE UNIVERSE.

I figured as much. HEY, UNIVERSE! LoOKin' sharp.

Try these activities on for size! You'll be weird in no time.

#1 Make up a strange Hemka-like language with your friends. Be bold! Use it in public for everyone to hear. You might get a few odd looks.

#2 Spend one whole day in total silence! Go lots of places but don't speak to anyone. You can only communicate in smiles. Big smiles, little smiles, **LOTS AND LOTS OF SMILES!** But no talking.

#3 Write the craziest story you can think of and make it about YOU. Are you a cosmic mechanic who also works as a hairdresser? Maybe you're a pig who becomes the leader of a planet where ice cream cones are like money? **MAKE IT CRAZY**.

#4 Use whatever arts and crafts you can find around your house to build a totally new kind of pet. Give it a name, a backstory, and show it off to your friends and family.

#5 Become a **Moonflower!** You'll have to live on a moon, on the edge of space, surrounded by cheerful (and not so cheerful) creatures while you protect a moon from a giant muck monster that wants to eat your home. Sound good?

I'm feeling WEIRDER ALREADY.

MOOD BOARD!
·········· ORANGE ··········

Want to know what makes me weird? There are too many things to count! But I'll tell you this— I love them all! Except maybe that one weird thing on my toe. What's the deal with that?

Oh, who am I kidding? I even love that weird toe thing. It's part of what makes me, me!

Here's what I want to know:
What makes you weird?

_____

_____

_____

_____

Make the weirdest face ever. Now draw it!

THE BIG BAD LURKS

PROTECTING YOUR MOON

Protecting a moon is a **HUGE** responsibility for a Moonflower. You have to protect the whole moon, and all the things living on it, too!

That responsibility's even tougher when **YOU HAVE NO IDEA WHAT YOU'RE DOING!** But when the odds are stacked against you (and, let's be honest, they are **A LOT**), you've got to **GATHER YOUR FORCES** (also known as friends, squishy and otherwise) and **FIGHT, FIGHT, FIGHT!** No matter what happens, **STICK TOGETHER!**

I feel like we've really gotten to know one another during this experience, Hanazuki. You inspire me to be my best self. You've also inspired another **DANCE BREAK!** Come on, Hanazuki, shake your Moonflower!

WOOO HOOO!

YOU AND HANAZUKI WIN THE DAY!

Well, Dazzlessence Jones, I think there might be a few more Moonflowers out there than there were when we started. Our work here is done.

Not so fast, Hanazuki! There's always more to do!

Of course. Until we meet again, Universe! In the meantime, find your mood powers, Moonflowers!